My Friend
the
Piano

For my mother
— C.C.

For Betsy, who composes
— K.H.

Acrylic paints on paper were used for the full-color illustrations.
The text type is 16-point Novarese Medium.

Text copyright © 1998 by Catherine Cowan
Illustrations copyright © 1998 by Kevin Hawkes

Published by Lothrop, Lee & Shepard Books
an imprint of Morrow Junior Books
a division of William Morrow and Company, Inc.
1350 Avenue of the Americas, New York, NY 10019
www.williammorrow.com

Printed in the United States of America.

10 9 8 7 6 5 4 3 2 1

Library of Congress Cataloging-in-Publication Data

Cowan, Catherine.
My friend the piano / by Catherine Cowan; illustrated by Kevin Hawkes.
p. cm.
Summary: When a piano which loves to play "symphonies" but refuses to practice is sold
for use as a storage chest, it escapes with the help of a child and plunges into the sea.
ISBN 0-688-13239-1 (trade)—ISBN 0-688-13240-5 (library)
[1. Piano—Fiction. 2. Music—Fiction. 3. Sound—Fiction.] I. Hawkes, Kevin, ill.
II. Title. PZ7.C8347Mu 1998 [E]—DC20 93-37437 CIP AC

My Friend the Piano

BY CATHERINE COWAN

ILLUSTRATED BY KEVIN HAWKES

LOTHROP, LEE & SHEPARD BOOKS • MORROW

NEW YORK

I<small>F YOU GO TO</small> S<small>YMPHONY</small> R<small>OCK</small>, you will see where my friend the piano escaped to the sea with my music safe inside.

It all started the first time I hauled myself onto the piano bench, touched the keys, and began to compose. As I grew and my feet reached the pedals, my music swelled with passion. At times the piano wept. At other times it shrieked with laughter.

One day Mother announced it was time I took lessons and learned how to play. "But I know how to play," I said.

"That is *not* playing," said Mother. "It's noise."

The lessons proved a disaster. The piano groaned over practice pieces, sulked at fingering exercises, and screamed when I played scales. Then it fell silent.

"I don't hear you practicing," Mother called.

"I can't," I told her. "The piano won't play."

Mother came into the room. She looked at the piano. She looked at me. "Play," she said. My fingers came down on the keys. Nothing. Not a sound.

"Get up," said Mother. She sat on the bench and looked at the piano.

She worked her hands, flexing her fingers, then stretched her arms. Having paid homage to the keyboard, she touched the keys. And the piano filled the air with music. While Mother waited, I began to practice. But my friend wouldn't play scales for me.

Mother decided to drill me. She pushed each finger down in turn on the proper key. The piano moaned, and all the notes went flat. A man came and tuned the piano. But when Mother drilled me again, the piano lost its tune: Now all the notes were sharp.

This was a terrible time for me. Mother wouldn't allow any composing until I had finished practicing, and the piano wouldn't let me practice. Every time I tried, it either fell silent or went out of tune.

The piano tuner came again. He lovingly tightened each string and adjusted every hammer. When he tested it, the piano played perfectly. He went away. I sat down to practice and every note sounded flat.

The man came a dozen times in a dozen days. Finally Mother asked him to wait while I practiced. The notes went sharp, then flat; then three notes sounded for every key I touched.

"It's an old piano," said the man. "Since your house overlooks the sea, it probably suffers from the damp."

Mother said I wasn't to practice. She needed time to think. While she was thinking, I decided to compose. I started out quietly enough. But soon the feeling of the music carried me away. Waves crashed; car horns honked; the piano laughed with glee.

Mother came into the room. "What *are* you doing?" she asked.

"I'm not practicing. I'm composing. The piano likes my symphonies, but it doesn't like playing scales."

"Composing!" said Mother. "That's not composing. That's not even music."

"Yes, it is," I told her. "It's the sound of a traffic jam. It's a part of the piece."

"It's noise," she said. "Now close the cover and leave the piano alone."

Mother decided to sell the piano and buy a new one. She put an ad in the newspaper, offering the piano for sale. But every time someone came to look at it and sat down to play, the piano lost its tune. Father said it was the coastal weather. Mother said it was an antique. I said none of that was true: The piano was my friend and wouldn't play for anyone but me.

We didn't sell the piano, and I couldn't practice, so every afternoon I composed a new symphony.

Then Grandmother called to say she wanted to come and live with us. Mother looked at the music room. "We'll make this her bedroom," she said.

"Good. Then we can move the piano into my room," I said.

"No," said Mother. "The piano will have to go."

Father put a new ad in the newspaper. FREE PIANO, it read. A lady with
a shop in town came to see the piano.
She liked it. And she liked the price. If
we would deliver it, she would take it.
I told her it wouldn't stay in tune. But
she didn't care. She planned to tear
its guts out, paint it green and pink
and blue, and use it as a storage
chest.

"You can't do that!" I cried.

"If she'll take the piano," Father
said, "she can do whatever she wants
with it." And he agreed to deliver the
piano the following day.

I pleaded with my parents to let me
keep it. "Grandmother can have my
room. I'll move in with the piano."

"No," said Mother. "I like my sleep.
I'm not about to risk you banging
away and making a racket some
night." Mother doesn't like symphonies. She prefers Bach.

Father decided to save money and move the piano himself. He ordered me to help. We started rolling it down our driveway. I felt miserable.

It rolled along nicely until we neared the end of the drive. Father wanted to go right. The piano wanted to go straight.

Father told me to get around front and block it. Then he shouted for Mother to come and help. I put my back to the piano and braced my feet to keep it from rolling over me, but I couldn't stop it.

That was when the idea came to me.

"I'll save you," I whispered to the piano. "Only you have to do exactly as I say." Pianos can't nod, and pianos can't speak, but I felt it hesitate.

"Turn to the right," I whispered. The piano eased to the right.

Mother came running down the driveway but tripped, and Father moved to catch her.

"Now!" I shouted, and jumped onto the piano. We were off like a flash.

At the next turn I screamed, "Left, left!" The piano swung left, and we plunged down the hill.

People saw us whizzing by and ran out to the street. They waved their arms. "Jump!" they yelled. "Jump!" But I wouldn't jump! I couldn't let the piano go crashing into a tree.

We raced along, faster and faster. As we passed the park, my friends came running from their ball game. Some of them chased after us, calling, "I want to ride, too," but none of them could catch up.

Ahead of us was a highway—packed with cars. The traffic light turned red, and I screamed for the piano to stop, but it couldn't stop. We skidded around the corner and whizzed along beside the cars until we reached a crosswalk. "Look out!" I screamed.

The pedestrians jumped clear, except for one old woman. She stood right in the middle of the street, pointed with her cane, and ordered us to stop. The piano refused, and we barreled across.

We shot up a rise on the opposite side and careened through a parking lot on the cliff. I steered the piano to a gap in the barrier wall. We zipped through and plowed up a hedge of azaleas. As we zoomed under a cypress, the front end fell into space.

I grabbed for the tree, caught a branch, and clung. I looked down. My friend the piano was in the sea. The waves swept in, and tenderly lifting it, they carried it away.

Though Grandmother never came, things have changed. Now I compose concertos for pots and pans. Father says he likes my music, but I notice he plays a lot of baseball instead of watching it on TV. And Mother has taken up jujitsu.

In the evening, I go with her to sit and listen at Symphony Rock. Mother still says she likes Bach. But the music I love drifts in on the breeze. It's the susurrous sound of my symphonies sailing far distant seas, safe in my friend the piano.